Dumper Truck Dash

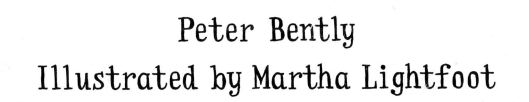

Peter Bently

Illustrated by Martha Lightfoot

QED
Powys

Beaver climbs into Dumper Truck's cab
and starts the **powerful** engine.

A new Town Hall is being built because
the old one was **damaged** in a fire.

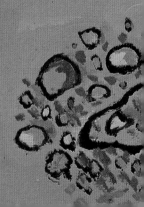

Dumper Truck is helping to **clear** the building site.

Dumper Truck and Beaver are going to **recycle** as much of the old material as possible.

They take a load of **scrap metal**
to the bicycle factory.

Then they take a load of **soil** to the new park.

Back on the building site, Bulldozer clears the old building into big piles.

CRUNCH!

Digger **picks up** rubble in its scoop...

CRASH!

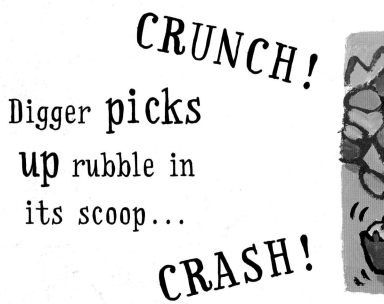

...and **drops** the rubble into Dumper Truck's strong tipper.

They **fill** in the new Town Hall's foundations. Beaver pulls the lever and Dumper Truck's tipper slowly tilts up and the rubble pours out.

WHIRR!

"Well done," says Beaver. "Let's get another load."

It starts to rain. Beaver turns on Dumper Truck's **windscreen wipers** so he can see through the window.

Dumper Truck is **big and tough** and can work
in any weather. This means Beaver can move lots
of rubble very quickly.

Now the rain is **pouring** down.
A police car arrives.

NEE-NAW
NEE-NAW!

POLICE

POLICE

"The river is about to burst its banks,"
says the police officer. "The flood will head this way!
Everyone must **leave** the building site."

From high up in Dumper Truck's cab, Beaver can see where the river is close to **overflowing.**

"I have an idea!" he says.

Digger **helps** load Dumper Truck with the rest of the rubble.

When the tipper is **full**, Beaver and Dumper Truck set off.

"That's the **wrong** way!" cries the police officer.
"You're heading for the river!"

"**Don't worry,**" says Beaver.
"We know what we're doing!"

Beaver and Dumper Truck **hurry**
towards the river.

The heavy rain has made deep puddles, but Dumper Truck's **huge wheels** keep the engine out of the water.

Dumper Truck's **big tyres** stop them from skidding in the mud.

Beaver reaches the riverbank.
He sees where the water
is starting to **overflow**.

Beaver **carefully**
backs up and pulls the lever.

Dumper Truck **tips** the rubble into place.

Beaver and Dumper Truck watch as the rubble **stops** the river from overflowing. "We did it!" cries Beaver.

Back at the building site everyone is very pleased.

"Well done, Beaver!" they cry.

"Thanks," says Beaver. "But Dumper Truck is the real hero. Well done Dumper Truck!"

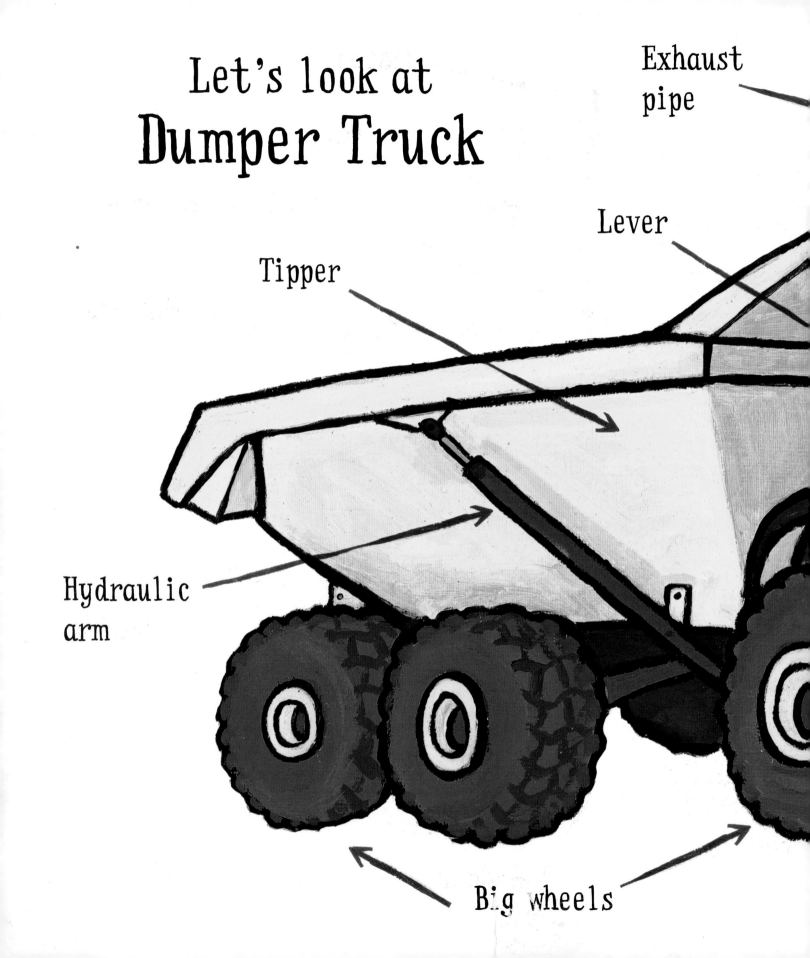

Let's look at
Dumper Truck

Exhaust pipe

Lever

Tipper

Hydraulic arm

Big wheels

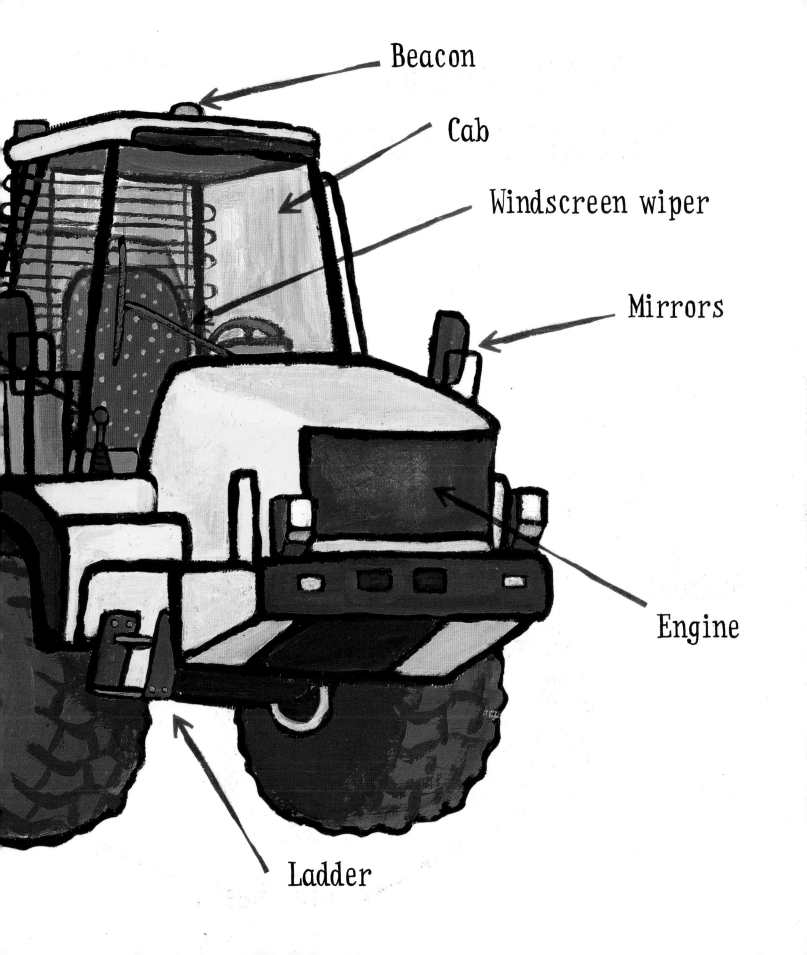

Beacon

Cab

Windscreen wiper

Mirrors

Engine

Ladder

Other Building Machines

Wrecking
crane

Cement mixer

Bulldozer

Digger

For my mum and dad, with love. M.L.
For Eli. P.B.

Designer: Plum5 Limited
Project Editor: Lucy Cuthew
Editorial Assistant: Tasha Percy

First published in the UK in 2013 by
QED Publishing
A Quarto Group company
230 City Road
London EC1V 2TT

www.qed-publishing.co.uk

A catalogue record for this book is available from the British Library.

ISBN: 978 1 78171 091 3

Printed in China